ALFIE
~ THE ~
WEREWOLF

More books in the series

Full Moon

Coming soon . . .

Silvertooth
Wolf Wood
The Evil Triplets
Werewolf Secrets

ALFIE THE WEREWOLF
Birthday Surprise

Written by
Paul van Loon

Translated by
David Colmer

Illustrated by
Hugo van Look

Hodder
Children's
Books

A division of Hachette Children's Books

For Hadjidja and Manisha

1

Seven

It was the middle of the night and Alfie shot up in bed. For a second he didn't know what had woken him. Something important was happening, he could feel it. Something about him had changed, but what?

Suddenly a moonbeam shone through an opening in the curtains, right on Alfie's face. A silver line ran down his forehead, nose and chin. Then Alfie remembered: it was his birthday. Maybe this was a sign that he was turning seven at exactly this moment.

Seven years old. At last! Now he was

almost as old as Tim, who was already eight.

If I keep this up, thought Alfie, I'll catch up with him. Yesterday Tim was two years older than me. Now he's only one year older.

He was so excited he had to get up. He took his glasses from the bedside cabinet, put them on, threw off the duvet and jumped out of bed.

Tingling with a new feeling, Alfie walked through the room. Behind the curtain, the window was partly open and the noises of the night drifted into Alfie's room – chirping crickets, croaking frogs, little animals rustling over the grass and under the bushes – noises he had never heard so clearly and distinctly before. They sounded like they were being amplified over a speaker. He smelt the grass and the bushes.

For a moment he thought of his parents. He always thought of them on his birthday. He wondered where they were now. Did they know he had already turned seven?

His parents were mysterious strangers that he no longer remembered. He didn't know why he always thought of them on his birthday.

Suddenly Alfie felt itchy. Terribly itchy all over his body. Scratching didn't make any difference. Maybe some fresh air would help?

He slid open the curtain.

There was someone on the other side of the window. A figure was standing there.

Alfie screamed and jumped back.

2

Howl

The figure jumped back too at exactly the same time.

For a second Alfie just stood there without moving. Then he worked it out.

How stupid! What an idiot. Scared of his own reflection in the window. He had acted like a six-year-old, not like someone who was already seven. He hadn't recognized himself in the dark glass. No wonder he'd given himself a fright.

Alfie sniggered. He was glad nobody else had seen him.

He opened the window wide and breathed in the night air. The moon cast a magical glow over the garden.

Alfie looked up. It was the most beautiful night he'd ever seen. There were millions of stars in the sky, all twinkling and sparkling like decorations hung up for his seventh birthday.

The moon was full and shining brightly. Alfie couldn't keep his eyes off it. The moonlight shone on his face and gleamed on the lenses of his glasses.

Alfie had never known that you could feel moonlight, but he felt it now. It was cool, but it made his skin glow at the same time. The light scampered over his nose and lips like a mouse's feet, then slid down his neck and into his pyjamas. It was as if the light had crept into his skin and was flowing right through him like a shower of moonbeams. It felt good and Alfie felt happy, even though he was still itchy all over.

He leant on the window ledge with both hands and opened his mouth wide, as if to drink the moonlight. He felt a terrible urge to shout out something to the moon. Something like, 'Hello, moon, I turned seven tonight. And that is so itchy!'

Then a sound he had never made before came up out of his throat. A loud, scary howl like a noise an animal would make.

Alfie clapped his hand over his mouth in horror. Had that sound really come out of his mouth? He couldn't believe it.

Confused, he looked up at the moon and couldn't stop himself from opening his mouth. Once again, Alfie howled at the moon. It was a sad sounding cry. 'Oww-owwwww!'

With great difficulty he clamped his jaws shut. He couldn't work it out. What was happening? Was this normal? Did your voice change the moment you turned seven? Was it breaking already? Tim hadn't warned him about this.

Alfie looked down at the window ledge where his two hands were resting. He almost screamed, but just managed to cover his mouth with his hands.

Something terrible had happened.

He no longer recognized his own hands.

3

No!

Alfie's hands were suddenly covered with white hair and he had grown long, sharp nails.

No matter how much Alfie stared at them, the hair and nails didn't disappear. His feet were the same: white and hairy with sharp nails.

My hands have turned into paws! I've grown claws!

Alfie started to panic.

He turned back to the open window and saw that his reflection in the glass was very dark. He looked strange and deformed. His hair was wild and his ears stuck up on the sides of his head like pointy tufts. Thick hair bulged up out of his sleeves and the collar of his pyjama top, as if he was wearing a thick fur coat.

This is terrible, thought Alfie. Is that me, with all that hair? He looked around desperately, not knowing what to do.

Nothing like this had ever happened to him before. What if someone saw him like this? The thought made him feel trapped.

Suddenly his pyjamas were much too tight. He tugged at the top, sending the buttons flying. *Rip, tear* – he kicked and tore the pyjama bottoms off his legs. Free at last.

Alfie growled softly. He still felt trapped in the room. The four walls suddenly felt like a prison.

The moon smiled at him through the window as if to say, 'Come on out, Alfie. Taste freedom.'

Alfie leant on the window ledge again with his front paws. His tail wagged back

and forth longingly. Tail?

Alfie looked back over his shoulder. He hadn't imagined it.

A fluffy white tail was attached to his bottom.

Suddenly there was a quiet knock on the door.

4

A Blur

The strange noises coming from Alfie's room had woken up Tim, whose bedroom was next to Alfie's. For a while now he had been lying in bed, listening.

Maybe they're only dream noises, he thought.

But then he heard it again: a strange howl.

Alfie Span was Tim's best friend and Tim loved him like a brother. Four years ago, Alfie's parents had disappeared. They had left suddenly one night, without any warning or note. No one knew where Mr and Mrs Span had gone. It was a big mystery. Since then, Alfie had lived with Tim and his parents.

Tim climbed out of bed, tiptoed over the landing and stopped outside Alfie's room. Carefully, he pressed his ear against the door and heard rustling and shuffling noises. He knocked on the door quietly.

No answer.

Tim knocked again.

'Pssst, Alfie, what are you doing?'

All at once it went dead quiet behind the door.

That's strange, thought Tim. Was something the matter with Alfie?

Suddenly he felt scared and worried.

He turned the door handle and pushed open the door.

A gust of wind blew in his face. The window was wide open and the room was lit up with bright moonlight.

Tim grew even more scared.

Something was wrong.

Tim looked around the room. Alfie's bed was empty. Where was Alfie? His pyjamas were lying on the floor.

Tim picked them up. What were they doing on the floor? And why were they torn?

Nothing made sense.

Tim leant out of the window and looked into the garden. The trees and garden furniture cast black shadows in the silver moonlight. But the garden was dead quiet too.

Suddenly Tim heard a sound and spun around.

Something was moving in a dark corner of the room.

'Alfie?'

No answer, just a soft growl.

'Alfie?'

Tim shuffled towards the door.

I'd better wake up Mum and Dad, he thought.

He reached for the door handle, but was too slow. It was as if the shadows exploded.

In a flash, Tim saw a white blur moving towards him.

'*Wrow!*'

He fell over backwards and felt warm breath on his face.

5

A White Wolf

Tim's eyes were wide open but his brain couldn't believe what he was seeing. There was something very hairy on top of him.

It looked like a wolf. A white wolf. Not a great big one, but a fairly small one, with big, round, gleaming eyes.

Tim screwed up his own eyes, too scared to look.

Paws pressed down on his shoulder as the wolf panted in his face.

A terrible thought came to him. Alfie had disappeared. Only his pyjamas were left in

the room. That could mean only one thing:
this strange wolf had eaten Alfie. It had
swallowed him whole. And now it's my turn,
thought Tim.

The wolf sniffed at his face. Tim wanted
to yell for help, but was too terrified to move.
No noise came out of his throat.

Then something very strange happened.
Carefully, the wolf pressed its nose against
Tim's throat and licked him very gently on
the cheek with its rough tongue.

'Tim,' the wolf whispered. 'Don't be scared,
it's me.'

Cautiously, Tim opened his eyes. He was
too astonished to speak. What was happening

here was impossible. A talking wolf was sitting on his chest. A wolf that sounded like Alfie with a growling voice.

Wolves can't talk, thought Tim. And they definitely can't talk with Alfie's voice. So this can't possibly be real.

The wolf nuzzled Tim's ear.

'Tim, it's me, honest,' it said.

It turned its head so that the moon shone straight on its face.

Only now did Tim see that the big shiny eyes were just Alfie's glasses.

'Alfie? Is that you? It can't be. What's happened to you? You're so . . . hairy! Your mouth is enormous and your ears are huge!'

The wolf whimpered softly. 'I don't know. I changed.'

'I can see that,' Tim said.

'What do I do now?' Alfie asked. His voice sounded miserable.

'Get off me to start with,' Tim said. 'It's hard to think with a wolf on top of you.'

'Oh, sorry,' Alfie said as he got off Tim's chest.

'That's better.' Tim sat on the floor next to Alfie. 'Now tell me what happened.'

Alfie hung his head.

'I woke up and the moon was shining in my face. Then I thought, Yippee, I'm seven.' He whimpered softly. 'The next thing I knew, I had paws and a tail.'

Tim picked his nose thoughtfully, then flicked the bogey out of the window.

Outside, the moon was now clearly visible.

Suddenly Tim clapped his hands together. 'Hey, I get it. You're a werewolf. Cool!'

Alfie lifted his head and gave Tim a questioning look. 'I'm a what?'

'A werewolf. That's a person who changes into a wolf when there's a full moon.' Tim jumped up. 'This is so cool! I bet I'm the only kid around who has a real werewolf. That's heaps better than an ordinary pet.'

Alfie whimpered louder. 'A pet? I'm not a pet. I don't want to be a pet! And I don't want to be a werewolf either.'

Alfie looked so miserable that Tim wished he'd kept his mouth shut. Of course Alfie wasn't a pet – what a stupid thing for him to say.

'Maybe it will get better by itself,' Tim said. 'Like chickenpox or measles.'

'And if it doesn't?'

'Then . . . then I'll help you. I'll . . .'

Tim stopped talking and stared at Alfie.

Alfie crouched down and bunched up his shoulders.

'What are you doing now?' Tim asked.

'I . . . I can't help it. I can't breathe in here. I have to go outside.' Alfie sprang through the air. He just took off and flew over Tim and out through the open window, all the way down from the first floor in one leap.

Tim rushed to the window.

'Alfie, don't go!' he shouted.

6

Free as a Bird

Alfie ran through the shadowy streets, past the dark houses. The wind ruffled his coat. High above were the moon and the stars. And all was dead quiet.

Alfie felt amazing! It was brilliant running as free as a bird . . . as free as a wolf, while everyone was asleep. No one knew that a white werewolf was running down the street.

There was a black cat sitting on a wall, its green eyes glittered like emeralds. Alfie slowed down and stood up straight.

'*Wrow*, cat. You out late too?'

The cat started to spit. It arched its back and bristled its tail. It shot off the wall and disappeared into the garden on the other side.

Great, thought Alfie, it wants to play. I'll join in.

With a big jump he flew over the wall.

Whoops! He had landed in bushes and thistles. No cats in sight. The branches got caught in Alfie's coat and thorns jabbed his paws.

'Ow, ooh, ah!' Alfie hopped up and down on his hind legs, whimpering from the pain.

Behind a window, a light flashed on.

Alfie wrenched his tail loose from a tangle of troublesome thistles. He bashed aside branches with his forepaws.

A loud cackling suddenly erupted.

Chickens.

Alfie turned his head towards the noise.

There was a tumbledown chicken coop in the garden. The chickens cackled like mad things.

Alfie leered at the chickens and licked his

lips. Then he leapt over to the chicken coop and tore open the door. The cackling grew even louder.

Suddenly the front door of the house opened.

Yellow light from the hall shone into the garden, right on the chicken coop. A woman was standing in the doorway in a nightie. She was wearing a silly-looking hat with feathers sticking out.

'Who's there?'

Then her mouth fell open.

There, at her chicken coop, was a wolf.

A little white one with glasses on its snout.

The woman started screeching.

1

Blood

A thud made Tim wake up with a start.

He sat up and peered around. Where was he?

Oh yeah, in Alfie's room, Tim suddenly remembered. He had been sitting here waiting for Alfie to come back, then fallen asleep for a moment.

A moment?

He looked at the light creeping into the room over the windowsill. It wasn't moonlight any more. It was the pale light of early morning, which meant the night was almost over. He must have been asleep for hours.

Alfie! he thought suddenly.

It was already morning and Alfie wasn't back yet. Maybe something terrible had happened. He was just starting to panic when he heard another thud. Then a blur appeared in front of the window, momentarily blocking the light. In the next instant Alfie shot in through the open window and landed flat on his stomach, his four legs outstretched. He lay on the floor, panting, with his tongue hanging out of his mouth and his glasses crooked on his head.

'Phew,' he gasped. 'Jumping down is a lot easier than jumping up. I smashed into the wall twice.'

Tim looked at Alfie and swallowed. He still wasn't used to the idea of Alfie being a werewolf. But it was the other things Tim saw that sent a shiver down his spine. There were clods of mud, twigs and feathers stuck to Alfie's fur. White feathers and black feathers. But worst of all was the blood. Blood stuck to the corners of his mouth and smeared red all over his white muzzle.

8

A Monster

'What happened?' Tim whispered. 'You look terrible. Where have you been? Did you fall over or run into a lamppost or something?'

Alfie didn't answer. He was still lying flat on the floor, panting. He looked up with one eye. Tim saw that his eyes hadn't changed. They were ordinary human eyes.

Alfie whimpered softly. He started to paw the ground. His tail swished over the floor. Then his body started jerking.

The room became brighter as dawn slipped into day, and in the light of morning

Alfie started to change back.

Tim watched open-mouthed as he saw Alfie's muzzle shrink. The pointed ears shrank too. His wolf's head became a human face and the white fur seemed to mysteriously dissolve. The sharp claws disappeared. Paws turned into hands and feet. Until finally Alfie was lying there on the floor. Alfie Span. Without a tail, in the nude.

Alfie gazed up at Tim. Then he looked at his hands and legs and feet. 'Tim, I'm me again!' He gathered up his torn pyjamas and quickly pulled them on. 'It's over, isn't it, Tim?'

Tim nodded. 'I think it is, thank goodness. But . . .'

Alfie heard the strange tone in Tim's voice.

'What is it, Tim?'

'Well,' Tim hesitated. 'What I'm worried

about is the blood . . .'

'Blood?' whispered Alfie. 'What blood?'

'On your jaws – I mean, on your mouth. Where's it from, Alfie?'

Alfie wiped his chin and looked at the red stripe on his fingers. His eyes widened with horror.

'And those feathers,' Tim continued. 'How'd you get those feathers in your hair?'

He plucked a few white feathers out from behind Alfie's ears.

Alfie froze. 'Oh, now I remember. There was a woman, Mrs Chalker, you know. She always wears a hat with feathers. Uh-oh . . .' Alfie's muscles turned to jelly. His knees buckled underneath him.

Tim grabbed his arm.

'What do you mean, Alfie? What's wrong?'

Alfie shook his head and collapsed on the bed. He started sobbing loudly. 'I'm so ashamed. I'm a horrible monster, Tim. I ate her up. I'm a wild, ravenous beast . . .'

He didn't get a chance to say any more as

there was a quiet knock on the door. Then
someone pushed it open.

'Alfie, happy birthday!'

Tim's mum and dad were standing there in
their dressing gowns, with beaming faces.

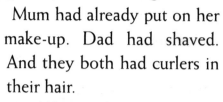

Mum had already put on her
make-up. Dad had shaved.
And they both had curlers in
their hair.

Alfie quickly wiped away
his tears. He didn't want
them to see that he had been
crying. He didn't want them
to know what had happened.
What a disaster of a birthday!

9

A Ghost

Mum spread her arms, walked over to Alfie, hugged him and gave him a big kiss on the cheek.

Alfie didn't move a muscle. He hoped she wouldn't notice the blood on his chin.

'Oh, look, silly me,' she exclaimed. 'I've smeared lipstick all over your face.' She grabbed a tissue and wiped Alfie's chin clean. 'There, that's better,' she said.

Dad gave Alfie a kiss, grabbed his hand, and shook it up and down so hard that Alfie's torn pyjama top slid off his shoulders.

'Happy birthday, Alfie. Wow, you're really big now you're seven. It's high time you got some new pyjamas.'

'Definitely,' Mum said. 'You've grown out of them overnight.'

Dad nodded, making the curlers dance on his head. 'Yes, Alfie, when you turn seven, everything changes.'

Mum clapped her hands. 'Come on downstairs, boys. First the present. Then the cake.'

Mum and Dad walked out of the room.

Behind their backs, Tim and Alfie looked at each other. It was incredible. They hadn't noticed a thing.

The living room was decorated with streamers.

Mum and Dad sang 'Happy Birthday' at the top of their voices – out of tune, but very lovingly.

Now and then Alfie had to choke back a tear. Not because they were being so nice to him, but because he was so upset about what he had done.

Mum and Dad had bought him roller blades, like he'd always wanted, but it didn't cheer him up.

How could you have a good time if you were a werewolf and had just eaten someone up whole?

I'll never be happy again, thought Alfie. That's my punishment.

'Just pretend,' Tim whispered. 'Act like nothing's wrong.'

Alfie did his best to look cheerful, but he couldn't stop thinking about Mrs Chalker.

Mum had made a big strawberry cream cake. They all got a piece on a plate with a silver fork. Alfie loved strawberry cream cake, but the thought of eating some now was more than he could bear. He imagined the pieces of cake going down his throat and landing on top of Mrs Chalker.

Just looking at the blood-red strawberries on the cake made him feel sick.

For some reason he didn't even dare to pick up the silver fork.

'Eat up, Alfie,' Mum said. 'Or don't you feel like any of this super-scrumptious strawberry cream cake?'

Dad winked at Alfie. 'I'll eat it if you don't want it. I'm as hungry as a wolf.'

Alfie went white and Tim choked.

Fortunately the doorbell rang just at that moment.

'You get it, Alfie,' Dad said with his mouth full. 'It's probably for you.'

Alfie jumped up. He walked into the hall and opened the front door.

He leapt back.

There was a ghost at the door.

10

Fearless

Alfie screamed and ran back into the living room. He slammed the door shut.

'What's wrong, Alfie?' Dad asked. 'Who is it?'

Alfie gasped for breath and pointed at the hall. He couldn't speak. Tim gave him a strange look.

Finally, Alfie managed to say, 'G-g-ghost!'

Tim gave him an even stranger look. Then he started to laugh.

'A ghost?' he said. 'That I have to see.' He walked to the hall.

'No, Tim, don't!' Alfie shouted after him.

But Tim was already out in the hall with the living-room door closed behind him.

Alfie looked over to Mum and Dad, who were grinning as if it was an act the boys had planned in advance.

Alfie didn't know what to do. Out there, on the doorstep . . .

The living-room door banged open, Tim rushed in and slammed it shut again.

'A ghost,' he squeaked with a deathly pale face.

Mum and Dad exchanged a look.

'I guess that makes it my turn to go and investigate,' Dad said. 'Maybe it's a burglar.'

'Burglars don't usually ring the doorbell, sweetheart,' Mum said.

'Ah, that's true,' said Dad.

He slid his chair back and stood up.

But Tim and Alfie had blocked the door.

'Don't go, Dad,' Tim said.

'Please stay here,' Alfie begged.

'It's a—'

Dad nodded. 'I know. There's a grisly

ghost out there.'

He bent forward and whispered, 'But I'm not scared. Watch this.'

He walked over to the fireplace and took the iron poker off its hook.

'See! Armed with this, Sir William the Fearless can take on any ghosts. Out of the way, you two.'

Holding the poker in front of him like a sword, he pushed the boys out of the way and strode into the hall, closing the living-room door behind him.

11

Big Bad Wolf

'What's happening?' whispered Alfie.

He was listening with his ear pressed against the door. Tim was doing the same.

'Don't worry, boys,' Mum said. 'A ghost is no match for William the Fearless. I ought to know, I married him.' She giggled.

Tim and Alfie didn't think there was anything to giggle about. They did their very best to hear what was happening in the hall. Neither of them dared to go and have a look.

It seemed to take for ever. Then they

heard the front door slam. A horrible silence
followed. Tim and Alfie swapped terrified
glances. Suddenly they heard slow footsteps.
Then hard knocks on the living-room door,
followed by a hollow laugh. Tim and Alfie
leapt back.

Slowly the door swung open. It was
Dad. He knocked on the door again

with the poker and gave another hollow, ghostly laugh.

'Sorry, just joking, I couldn't resist,' he said. 'But you were right, it was a ghost.'

'I told you!' Tim blurted.

'Well, almost right,' Dad continued. 'Mrs Chalker is as ugly as a grisly ghost and just as nasty. And she haunts my nightmares.' He winked at Tim and Alfie.

Tim and Alfie looked at each other. Dad didn't get it. He didn't realize that he had just seen Mrs Chalker's ghost. Because Mrs Chalker was dead. She was inside Alfie's stomach – and now she had come back to haunt them.

'Chalker is worse than a ghost,' Dad said. 'She's a wolf in sheep's clothing, that's what she is. Throwing boots at cats in the night. Personally wringing her own chickens' necks when they stop laying eggs. I've seen her.'

Dad turned a bit red. He almost never got angry, but he couldn't stand Mrs Chalker. 'All she ever does is complain, the old witch. She just dropped by to tell me not to park my car in front of her house. It ruins her view. Bah!'

'You didn't hit her, did you, sweetheart?' Mum asked.

'Almost,' Dad replied. 'I came very close. I felt like giving her a whack with the poker. Yesterday she didn't want the boys playing football in the street either.' He shook his head. 'Do you know what else she said?'

'What?' Mum asked.

Dad suddenly burst out laughing. 'She said that a wolf ate one of her chickens last night.'

'What?' Tim and Alfie shouted together.

'A wolf!' Dad said. 'Here in town! That's how crazy she is.'

Alfie looked at Tim. Tim looked at Alfie.

'And you know what else she said?' Now Dad was hiccuping with laughter. 'She said the wolf was wearing glasses!' He slapped his knees with delight. His fit of anger was already over. 'Can you picture it, Alfie? A wolf in glasses! A short-sighted wolf!'

The lenses of Alfie's glasses steamed over.

Tim thumped him on the shoulder. 'Yes!' he whispered. 'She's alive! You didn't eat her up. It was only a chicken.'

It took a moment to sink in and then Alfie leapt up. He grabbed Tim and danced around the room.

'She's alive!' they sang. 'She's alive!'

Mum and Dad looked on in astonishment.

'What's got into those two?' asked Mum.

Dad shrugged.

The letterbox rattled in the hall.

'Birthday cards,' said Mum.

Alfie raced to the hall. There was a postcard lying on the doormat. Alfie picked it up and read: *'Happy birthday, Alfie. It starts at seven.'*

It didn't say who it was from. Who could have sent it? Maybe someone from my class at school, thought Alfie. He turned the card over to look at the picture on the other side.

For a second he held his breath.
It was a drawing of the Big Bad Wolf . . .

12

A Shadow

'Coincidence,' said Tim. 'Pure coincidence.'

'No such thing,' said Alfie.

He studied the postcard of the Big Bad Wolf with a gloomy expression.

'Someone knows what I am. I mean, they know I'm a werewolf.'

They were sitting in the square near their house with their roller blades on. The birthday celebrations were over. Some of Tim's uncles and aunts had come to visit, but there hadn't been any other kids. Besides Tim, Alfie didn't have any friends. For some reason no one ever paid him any attention. Alfie was small and inconspicuous. Maybe the other kids didn't even notice him.

He was worried about the postcard. It was bad enough being a werewolf. True, he hadn't eaten Mrs Chalker. That was a relief. But he still felt sorry for the chicken. And getting a mystery postcard from a mystery person didn't make things any better.

'I don't understand what you're so upset about,' Tim said. 'I wouldn't mind being a werewolf. It'd be cool. I'd get my own back on all the bullies.' He stared into space thoughtfully. 'Nick Bragman, for one. I'd sink my teeth into him if I could.' He rolled up his sleeve and rubbed a bruise on his upper arm. 'He gave me this last week.'

Suddenly he looked at Alfie. 'Hey, Alfie, that gives me an idea. Next time Nick does something, why don't you . . . I mean, you don't have to bite him to death or anything. Just give him a good scare. When you're . . . I mean, if you turn into a wolf again.'

Alfie jumped up. 'Are you crazy? I don't

want to change into a wolf again. I want to be normal like everyone else.' He threw the postcard of the Big Bad Wolf down on the ground and sped off on his roller blades.

'Alfie, wait,' Tim shouted. 'I didn't mean it like that.'

But Alfie had already disappeared around the corner. He was going as fast as he could. He was angry. Blazing with fury. But he was sad at the same time. Nobody understood him, not even Tim.

Tim thought being a werewolf was fun. It wasn't.

Suddenly Alfie missed his parents terribly. Not Tim's parents, but his real parents. They would have understood.

He could still hear Tim's voice from far behind but Alfie didn't stop. His legs went faster and faster, kicking out furiously. Left – right, left – right.

Around him the houses grew darker and darker. The streetlights flicked on. Under the lampposts Alfie's shadow glided along beside him.

Suddenly he jumped. His shadow was of a wolf. A wolf on roller blades. Horrified, Alfie looked down at his hands. Hairy white paws, with claws. It had happened again, without him even noticing. How was that possible?

Above the rooftops, the moon emerged from behind a cloud. Alfie groaned. A boy rode past on a moped and looked back in horror. *Hide* – I have to hide, thought Alfie. Otherwise they'll find out about me.

He looked around for a place to hide and saw the entrance to Green Park. He turned off the road and shot into the park. There were benches around the pond and under the trees and lots of dark places where no one could see him. Exhausted, Alfie flopped down on a bench under a big oak tree. In front of him a lawn sloped down to the pond. Ducks were asleep at the edge. There wasn't a single ripple and the water was as smooth as a window pane.

Hanging in that window was the reflection of the moon.

Alfie breathed heavily. Slowly he raised

his head. He had to look at the moon, whether he wanted to or not. His mouth opened wide of its own accord.

I don't want this, he thought desperately. I don't want to be different.

Then that horrible howl came out of his throat again. In the distance a few dogs started to bark. The ducks woke with a start and looked up.

Alfie hung his head, resting it on his paws. Tears glistened on his hairy white face. He was alone. Alone in the world.

'It's not easy at the start, is it?' said a raspy voice.

Behind the tree stood a dark figure, leaning on a walking stick.

13

Splash!

Alfie hid his face in his hands.

'Go away!' he growled. 'No one's allowed to see me.'

The grass rustled, leaves crackled.

'You don't have to be scared of me. I've seen plenty like you.'

Cautiously, Alfie spread his fingers a little, keeping his hands in front of his face. Slowly he turned his head. He peered at the tree through his fingers.

The man with the walking stick was standing there in the shadows without

moving. He was wearing a hat with a very wide brim and a long coat that fell all the way down to the ground. Alfie could only see the gleam of his eyes.

'What did you say?' Alfie whispered, to conceal the growl in his voice.

'Werewolves,' the man said. 'Do you think you're the only one? No one is ever the only one. No one is the only one who's blind, or poor. No one is the only one who's fat, or skinny, or alone, or freckly, or with braces, or in a wheelchair. There are always other people who are the same. You're never one of a kind!'

Slowly, Alfie lowered his hands. 'Do you mean . . . there are more like me?'

'That's what I'm telling you,' the man said. 'It's not as awful as you think.'

'I think it's terrible. I don't know any more when I'm normal and when I'm not. A minute ago I was just Alfie. And now suddenly I'm a werewolf again.'

The man raised his arm and pointed at the dark sky with his stick. 'It's because of the moon,' he said. 'It's very simple. All human beings have a wolf inside them. If they're angry, they start to growl. If they're sad, they start to howl. Only with some people, sometimes, the wolf really does comes out. That happens at full moon.'

Alfie looked up. The moon was a perfect circle. It was even bigger than it had been yesterday.

'That's not right,' he shouted. 'It's only a full moon now. But I turned into a hairball with claws yesterday too!' His voice was so angry the ducks took off in fright.

The dark figure behind the tree nodded in silence.

'That's right,' he said finally. 'For three nights every month you are able to turn into a werewolf. The full moon, the night before and the night after. Three nights in total.'

'Able?' shouted Alfie. 'You make it sound as if I have a choice. But I don't want it at all!' He stamped his foot furiously and lost his balance. He'd forgotten that he was still wearing roller blades.

Before he knew it, he was rolling down
the sloping lawn. He waved his arms to
regain his balance, but it didn't help. With a
loud splash, Alfie disappeared into the pond.

14

An Accident

Fortunately the pond wasn't very deep. Even a four-year-old could stand up in it. But the water was cold. Alfie resurfaced spluttering, with a frog sitting on his head.

'Oh dear,' sighed the man in the shadows. 'You're going to be hard work. On top of everything else, you're clumsy. You should have seen yourself hurtling down that slope.' The man made a strange cackling noise.

Alfie thought he was angry, but he wasn't. The man was shaking with laughter. He was leaning against the tree and the tree shook and the leaves danced on the branches as if the tree was laughing too. And suddenly Alfie had to laugh as well, despite the cold water. Rolling into a pond, arms waving – it was like something from a film.

Alfie's laughter pealed over the water. The frog joined in, croaking along enthusiastically.

'Thank goodness you can still laugh,' the man said suddenly. 'You should, too, because you should be happy with what you are. It's a gift. You shouldn't be scared of it. You just have to learn to control it.'

Alfie wiped some pondweed off his nose. 'What do you mean?'

The man in the shadows moved a little. Twigs snapped under his feet. 'I mean you have to learn to control yourself. Understand? If you don't, you'll do bad things. Biting people, maybe even eating them up.'

'Croak,' said the frog.

'I'm not talking to you, Mr Greenlegs,' the man said.

The frog fell quiet, then jumped into the water.

'Once you master the gift, you'll discover how special it is. You'll be able to run faster, jump higher and do all kinds of things you can't do as a human. Just be careful of silver. Silver is dangerous for werewolves.'

'How do you know all that?' Alfie asked.

The man walked over to the side of the pond. His face remained hidden under the broad brim of his hat. 'All in good time,' he said. 'Get out of the water first. Grab my stick, then I'll pull you out.'

When Alfie was back on dry land he asked, 'Who are you?'

The man laughed under his breath. 'Yesssss, I'm . . .'

Just then someone came into the park. Someone small, on roller blades. 'Alfie, are you here?' he called in the distance.

The man jerked aside.

Alfie turned and saw Tim racing over to him. He waved his arm.

'Alfie, phew. I was worried.' Tim stopped just in front of Alfie. 'Are you OK? Why are you all wet? Did you go for a swim or something?'

Alfie shook his head, spraying water everywhere. 'Accident,' he growled. 'I was talking to that man. He knows all about werewolves.'

'Man? What man?' Tim asked.

Alfie looked around but there was no one there.

15

Showering

'So who was this man in the park?' Tim asked. 'Where did he know you from? How does he know all that stuff about werewolves?'

'I don't know,' Alfie growled.

They turned into their street. Alfie was still a sopping-wet werewolf, so they had to roller-blade back through quiet streets and back lanes, keeping away from streetlights. It had been easy enough. No one paid them any attention. They were just two boys on roller blades. Nobody had noticed that one of them was a werewolf.

On the way Alfie had told Tim all about his talk with the man in the park.

'That guy could have been a kidnapper,' Tim said, 'or an escaped lunatic.'

Alfie looked up in fright. He hadn't thought of that. Either way, the man had acted very mysteriously. Alfie hadn't been able to see his face. And why had he run off the moment Tim appeared? There were lots of questions he couldn't answer.

'And how on earth can silver be dangerous?' Tim asked. 'What kind of rubbish is that?'

Alfie shrugged. He didn't understand it either.

'Anyway, first we have to get home,' Tim said. 'And then we have to smuggle you into your room.'

They went past Mrs Chalker's house. The chickens started cackling loudly in the coop. Behind a window in the house a shadow moved. The shadow of a hat with feathers.

'Keep going!' Tim said.

Tim and Alfie left their roller blades by the

back door and slipped inside. Quickly, Tim took off his coat and threw it over Alfie's head. That seemed the safest thing to do.

'Upstairs, fast,' Tim hissed. He pushed Alfie into the hall.

'Tim, is that you?' Dad shouted from the living-room.

Alfie froze.

Dad came out into the hall. He smiled at Tim and Alfie. His hair wasn't curly any more. He was wearing a long skirt with bright-coloured flowers on it that he had borrowed from Mum.

'Why has Alfie got your coat on his head?' he asked.

'He fell in the pond,' Tim answered. He couldn't come up with anything else at such short notice.

Alfie growled softly under the coat. Dad didn't seem to notice.

'You must be freezing, Alf,' he said, 'and sopping wet. Go and have a hot shower, quick.'

He went back into the living room without

saying another word. Tim shook his head as he watched him go.

'Sometimes I don't understand my father,' he said. 'That skirt doesn't suit him at all. Do you think other fathers dress up like that?'

'*Wrow!*' said Alfie.

He threw the coat over the coat rack and ran upstairs.

In the bathroom Alfie took off his wet clothes. His socks were torn. He hid them at the bottom of the pedal bin and turned on the shower. Only then did he look at himself in the mirror.

There he was. A naked, white werewolf with glasses. Hairy from head to toe. Is this really me? he wondered.

Alfie stood there motionless for a very long time, looking at himself.

An overwhelming feeling rose up inside him: hunger. And not just any kind of hunger. He felt like biting into something, sinking his teeth into a big slab of meat or a . . .

No! he thought. I mustn't bite anyone!

The lenses of his glasses had gone all misty.

The mirror grew hazy and Alfie's reflection disappeared. He laid his glasses on the edge of the washbasin. Then he stepped under the hot shower. The water gushed down over him. Clouds of steam filled the bathroom.

Alfie began scrubbing himself with a hard brush. Maybe the coat will disappear, he hoped. And maybe the hunger will disappear with it.

But that didn't happen.

Suddenly the door opened and Mum stepped in through the steam.

'Hello? What a fog, goodness! Alfie, are you in here?'

Alfie quickly covered his face with his paws. Tim's mother would see him and all would be revealed! There was nowhere to hide. Any moment now she would start screaming at the top of her voice. They would disown him and kick him out of the house. He'd never see Tim again. He'd roam the world all alone, and three times a month he'd be a werewolf howling at the moon.

Alfie waited, his face hidden behind his paws. Mum's arm appeared out of the mist. It looked tender and juicy.

Alfie suddenly felt the blood rushing through his veins.

He bared his teeth and growled softly.

16

A Fight

Mum's hand grabbed the shower curtain and pulled it shut.

'You need to keep the curtain shut, Alfie. You know that. Otherwise you'll get the floor all wet.'

Alfie didn't answer. Instead, a smothered sound came from behind the shower curtain.

'There's a clean towel on the laundry basket,' Mum said. 'Remember to open the window when you're finished.' Then she went away, leaving Alfie standing there, trembling, with his eyes shut.

He was holding his jaw clamped shut with his paws. His head moved wildly: up and down and from left to right, as if he was caught up in a terrible fight with himself. He growled and then whimpered softly.

Finally he calmed down and stood there for a long time, panting.

He couldn't believe it. Tim's mother hadn't seen a thing. She hadn't noticed that there was a werewolf in the shower. It was unbelievable.

It was also unbelievable that he had nearly bitten her arm off. He had almost done it! That would have been horrible.

Fortunately he had been stronger than his urge. It had taken a lot of effort, but he had been able to stop himself and now the hunger was gone completely. He could just feel the fright of it.

Alfie was shaking from the bottom of his feet to the tufts of his ears. He stayed standing there under the hot jets until his whole body had calmed down again.

As wet as a drowned rat, he stepped

out from under the shower. His limp ears hung down and water dripped off his tail on to the floor.

After a short search he found the big bath towel, with a picture of Mickey Mouse on it.

At least it's not the Big Bad Wolf, thought Alfie.

Quickly he rubbed himself dry and wrapped himself in the towel, pulling it up over his ears and peering out through an opening.

Completely covered up, he walked out on to the landing. He slipped into his bedroom.

A little later he was lying in bed with the blankets pulled all the way up. He kept his head under the pillow, so that Tim's mother wouldn't see him if she happened to come up to check on him.

He just wanted to go to sleep and not wake up again until this werewolf business was all over. He wished it was just a bad dream.

Maybe that's what it is, he thought, just before he fell asleep.

But maybe not.

I have to find that mysterious man. He can tell me more. He understands me.

Alfie decided to look for him the first thing tomorrow morning.

17

Noooo!

Alfie walked into the park. He had left home extra early that morning. Tim hadn't come with him. Alfie wanted to be alone. He thought that the man might not come out if someone else was with him.

Alfie walked to last night's bench and sat down. He looked at the pond and then at the tree.

'Pssst, you there?' he called.

It stayed quiet.

Alfie waited a while longer. Then he stood up. It was pointless, nobody was there.

Suddenly there was a rustling behind him. Alfie spun around. Was that a dark figure in the bushes? Or was it just the shadow of branches and leaves?

The cry of a baby made him jump. A lady with a buggy had turned into the park. Alfie looked in her direction and then back at the bushes. There was no more rustling. No dark figures appeared.

Of course not, thought Alfie. I was imagining things.

Suddenly he felt really stupid. What would the mysterious man be doing here in the bushes early in the morning? It was a good thing no one had heard him.

Alfie looked at his watch and got a shock. It was almost half past eight. He had to get to school like a rocket.

Just before the gate shut, he ran into the school playground. The kids were running and jumping, kicking and shoving, even spitting.

At least they're normal, thought Alfie. No one is like me.

For a moment he thought about what the mysterious man had said: 'No one is the only one.'

If you looked around he was right. There were various kids with braces. There must have been ten with freckles. And at least six with runny noses.

But no one is like me, thought Alfie. I'm sure there are no other werewolves wandering around here.

He thought of his parents again. Maybe *they* were like him. They'd have to be. He must have got it from someone. But if they were, why did they abandon him? He couldn't even remember what they looked like.

Suddenly he snapped out of his daydream. He could see two of the kids with runny noses approaching Tim on the other side of the playground.

They were both a head taller than him: Nick Bragman, first-class bully, and Rick, his buddy.

What did that creep want with Tim this time?

Cautiously, Alfie moved towards them.

'Check it out,' Nick yelled. 'Timmy's made of paper. If I blow, he falls over.' He blew on Tim and gave him a quick shove. Tim fell over.

'Good one,' Rick said.

Alfie shrank.

Tim didn't say anything. He scrambled up and tried to walk away, but Nick stopped him.

Without being noticed, Alfie crept closer.

Nick wiped the snot off his upper lip. 'Shall I blow again?' he said. 'Maybe this time Timmy will fly over the school roof.'

'Sounds cool,' Rick said.

'Watch this,' Nick grinned.

Alfie's legs were trembling. He was actually scared of those big boys, but they wanted to hurt Tim. Alfie felt an unknown rage rising up in him. He heard a strange rushing sound in his ears. It was as if a red haze appeared before his eyes.

He saw Nick grabbing Tim by the collar, blowing in Tim's face. Pulling his fist all the way back.

'Noooo!' roared Alfie.

18

Aaaah!

Alfie leapt forward as if he'd been launched with a rubber band. He slammed into Nick with a growl and wrapped his arms around the boy's legs.

Nick didn't fall over. He just stayed standing where he was.

Surprised, he looked down at Alfie. He moved his leg, as if trying to kick away a bothersome fly.

But Alfie didn't let go. He clasped Nick's legs tight and glared up at him.

'Leave Tim alone,' he growled.

Nick's eyes grew bigger. He looked over at his friend and burst out laughing. 'D'you hear that, Rick? This midget's telling me what to do.'

Rick nodded and laughed just as loud. 'I heard.'

Tim shuffled back and forth awkwardly. Nick was still holding him by the collar.

'Alfie, get out of here,' Tim hissed. 'They'll get you too.'

Alfie didn't let go. He kept looking up at Nick and growling.

'Look. It's all snarly,' Nick sniggered.

Rick was hiccuping with laughter. 'Maybe we should give him the treatment too,' he suggested.

Nick nodded. 'Good idea. Two wimps in one go.'

Tim tried to break free. The bullies were going to bash him first. And then Alfie.

'Stop wriggling,' Nick said. 'I— Aaaah!'

19

A Plan

Nick's shriek echoed over the playground. All the kids stopped what they were doing to look in the same direction.

Nick Bragman hopped across the playground on one foot. He was holding on to his other leg. A piece of his trousers had been torn off and the skin of his leg was dark red.

'I'm bleeding,' Nick wailed. 'He bit me.'

Alfie was squatting on the ground, panting heavily, with a piece of material between his teeth. Rick was staring at Alfie in disbelief.

Alfie spat out the material and stood up. Rick stepped back quickly.

Nick was still wailing and jumping around on one foot. The other kids were sniggering.

'I'll get you,' Nick said in a tearful voice. 'I'll get both of you, you wimps!'

Tim put his arm around Alfie's shoulders.

'You better be careful,' Alfie warned Nick. 'You think I'm a wimp. But at night I'm a wild, ravenous beast. Be careful at night!'

Tim and Alfie walked away together, Nick staring after them with his mouth hanging open. He raised his fist in the air.

'You wait, I'll get you,' he shouted again.

Tim and Alfie walked into the school building without looking back.

'Thanks,' Tim whispered.

Alfie was staring into space as if he hadn't even heard Tim. He still had a glowing feeling inside.

'Tonight it will happen again,' he said suddenly.

'What?' Tim asked.

'Tonight I'll change again.'

Tim looked at him quizzically. 'How do you know?'

Alfie looked up, as if searching the sky for the moon. 'I feel it. It's the third night. The wolf in me wants to come out. I felt it just then, when I attacked Nick. I was furious. I actually felt like I was a wolf. That's why I bit him, I guess.' He looked at Tim and grinned. 'Before, I was always too scared to defend myself. Especially against someone bigger than me. Standing up to him felt pretty good.'

Tim nodded and grinned back. 'You really showed him. But what now? Nick's going to want revenge, that's for sure.'

Alfie looked out at the playground where Nick was still wailing in pain. 'Don't worry,' he said. 'I've got a plan.'

20

Dressing Up

'Hey, where are you two going?' Tim's father asked.

Tim and Alfie were about to sneak out of the back door. All they could see of Dad was his bottom half. He was wearing swimming trunks. His head was in the cupboard under the kitchen sink. He was trying to fix something. Pliers, screwdrivers and other tools were spread everywhere.

'We're going roller-blading,' Tim said.

Dad peered at them from inside the cupboard. 'It's already dark outside.'

'That's what's so cool,' Tim said. 'Moonlight roller-blading. Haven't you ever heard of that?'

'Er, no – ouch!' Tim's father had hit his head. He rubbed his forehead with three fingers.

He gave Alfie a questioning look. 'Is it that cold out, Alfie?'

Alfie was wearing a big woolly hat pulled down over his head and ears, a scarf that covered half his face, gloves, and wellies up to his knees. All you could of him were his glasses.

'*Wrow!*' Alfie was too scared to say anything else, because the change had already started.

Dad backed out of the cupboard. He was wearing wellies and Mum's apron. 'With that scarf over your mouth I can't understand a word you're saying.'

Tim pushed Alfie towards the back door. 'Alfie's got that stuff on as a precaution,' he blurted. 'So it won't hurt as much if he falls over.'

Dad raised an eyebrow and rubbed the bump that had appeared on his forehead. 'If you ask me, a helmet and knee guards would be better. But that looks good too.'

'I'd rather wear a hat and scarf than an apron and swimming trunks,' Tim said.

Dad looked at him in astonishment. 'Don't you like this apron? And trunks are very practical if you're working with water.'

Tim nodded. 'Yeah, sure. Can we go now?'

Dad hesitated for a moment. 'OK, but be back within an hour. And remember . . .'

But Tim and Alfie were already gone. Tim's father shook his head, smiling. 'Alfie's taking after me,' he said. 'He can't get enough of dressing up either.' He lifted his apron by two corners. 'I think it's a cute little apron,' he mumbled. Then he dived back under the sink.

Tim and Alfie were hiding behind three wheelie bins.

'He lives there,' Tim said, pointing across

the lane at a house with a large garage. There was a bike lying on the front drive. Loud rap music was coming from a room upstairs.

'That's Nick's bike,' whispered Tim. 'And that's his room up there. Nick loves rap.'

Alfie nodded. 'Can you hold my stuff?' he growled. He took off the hat and scarf and pulled off his gloves. Alfie got undressed, quickly taking off his jeans, coat and everything else. His hairy paws, body and tail appeared.

He stretched, opened his jaws wide and spread his claws. The hairs of his white coat stood up on end.

Tim gulped for a second. Seeing your best friend with a tail, claws and sharp teeth wasn't something you got used to.

'Are you sure you want to go through with this plan?' he asked.

'*Wrow.*'

'OK, let's do it.'

They sneaked out from behind the bins. The street was now empty.

'Come on,' Tim whispered.

They rushed across the road, then walked up the garden path, past the bike. In Nick's room the rap music had stopped.

'Wait a sec,' Tim whispered.

He bent over to let down the tyres of Nick's bike.

'There,' he grinned. 'That's one–nil to us.'

Tim picked up a pebble from the path. Alfie was already standing under Nick's window.

'Ready?' Tim asked.

Alfie nodded. '*Wrow.*'

Tim brought his arm back and threw the pebble. It whizzed up and with a loud click it bounced off Nick's window.

CLACK!

Tim turned and sprinted back to the other side of the street.

21

Nick-ee!

Nick Bragman was sitting on his bed with one trouser leg pulled up past his knee, examining his leg. The teeth marks were clearly visible. That friend of Tim's had bitten right into him. The little four-eyed brat! But I'll get him back, thought Nick. Tomorrow I'll kick him from one side of the playground to the other – and Tim with him. They've got it coming! I'm not going to let them make a fool of me.

CLACK!

Nick jumped. What was that?

Something had banged against his window. He listened carefully, but it was dead quiet.

Nick walked over to the window and slid the curtain to one side. He looked out angrily. Who dared to throw stones at his window?

Behind the glass, Nick froze. He couldn't believe his eyes. Down there in the garden was something . . .

Something . . . terrifying.

Nick couldn't think of how to describe it. He could hardly think at all. It was a wolf. All white, with fluffy ears and claws and teeth.

But it couldn't be. That was impossible.

Nick rubbed his eyes with his fists and looked again.

The wolf was still sitting there. It was looking straight up at his room and snarling at him! And the strangest thing of all was that the wolf was wearing glasses. Glasses just like the ones the brat who bit him wore. The wolf opened its jaws and out of its throat

came a terrible howl that sounded like
'Nick-ee!'

Nick felt it through his whole body. He
was so scared he almost wet himself. And
suddenly he remembered what Alfie had said
in the playground: 'At night I'm a wild,
ravenous beast.'

Of course, that was impossible. But now
there was a wild, ravenous beast waiting for
him under his window.

In one dizzy moment Nick understood.
Alfie was a werewolf! And he was going to
get him and tear him to shreds.

Nick started shaking. His cheeks wobbled
and tears poured from his eyes. He was so

scared that he sank down on his knees by the windowsill and began to pray.

He squeezed his eyes shut. 'Please make the werewolf go away. I'll never bully anyone again. I'll always be a good boy. I'll even do the washing up. And I'll stop pinching the three-year-old girl next door.'

Slowly, he stood up straight. Would the beast be gone?

Nick counted to three, then opened his eyes. There were white paws on the window ledge.

Nick's mouth opened wide, but no sound came out of it. He was staring straight into the werewolf's eyes.

22

Ow! Ow!

Nick gasped for breath.

The werewolf was hanging off his window ledge. The monster opened its jaws and licked its teeth.

'*Wrow*, Nick-ee!'

A white paw reached out towards him. Long nails shot out of the paw and scraped over the glass. Nick cringed backwards, then turned and ran out of the room screaming, 'Mummy, help! There's a wolf in my room. It wants to eat me up.'

Tim was in the lane behind the bins.

He could hear Nick screaming for help through the window. Tim laughed so hard he almost fell over.

Alfie was fantastic. He was still hanging from the window ledge.

Alfie saw Nick run out of the room. Nick must have totally wet himself! He was still shouting, 'Mummy, Mummy!'

Time to get out of here, thought Alfie. He let go of the window ledge and dropped, landing neatly on all fours in the flowerbed. He shot out of the garden like a white stripe.

Tim was ready with his clothes.

'That was so cool,' Tim said. 'Quick, get dressed.'

Alfie pulled on his jeans. The hardest bit was getting them on over his tail, but with

Tim's help he managed. Alfie wormed his head into his jumper and pushed his front legs into the sleeves. He pulled the hat down over his head and put on the scarf. Then he pulled on his coat and finally his wellies.

'Ready?'

'*Wrow!*'

'Let's go.'

Calmly, they walked into the street. An enormous racket was coming through Nick's window.

'It's true!' Nick shouted. 'There was a wolf hanging off the window ledge. A werewolf!'

Tim and Alfie looked up.

They could see Nick and his mother through the window.

'You never believe me!' Nick screamed.

'Because you always lie,' Nick's mother shouted. 'And you're lying again now. One: there aren't any wolves around here. Two: werewolves don't exist. Three: they definitely don't go around hanging off bedroom window ledges.'

In a fury, Nick yelled a very nasty word.

Then he screamed, 'Ow!'

His mother had grabbed his ear and given it a squeeze.

Nick jumped back and looked out of the window. His face was red, as if he was about to cry.

Tim and Alfie waved cheerfully before disappearing around the corner.

'There! There they go!' Nick screamed.

'Liar!' his mother shouted, grabbing him by the ear again.

'Ow!'

Choking with laughter, Tim and Alfie ran into their own street.

'That was so cool, Alfie,' Tim said. 'Your plan was brilliant. You can have fun as a werewolf after all.'

'*Wrow.*'

Tim was right. As a werewolf, Alfie dared to do things he would never have done otherwise. Maybe being different from other people wasn't always such a bad thing. For the first time he felt all right as a werewolf.

All right? He felt fantastic.

He jumped in the air and kicked off his wellies. They weren't comfortable. He preferred to walk on his bare wolf paws. He caught the boots and threw them far away in front of him. They thumped down on the pavement further down the street.

'Don't do that,' Tim said. 'Someone will see—'

'Hey, you two, wait a minute,' screeched a voice.

23

Slippers

Mrs Chalker was standing at her garden gate. She was wearing her hat with the feathers again.

'She probably sleeps in it,' Tim whispered. 'Maybe it's even stuck to her head.'

Alfie didn't answer. 'My feet,' he growled through his teeth. 'If she sees my feet she'll scream blue murder.'

'Act normal,' Tim whispered. 'Then she won't notice. That old biddy's as blind as a bat.'

Mrs Chalker was carrying a big bag. She

must have just been to the supermarket. The bag was half open. It was stuffed full of leads, cables, lamps, horns and other strange devices.

'What did you buy?' Tim asked, looking into the bag inquisitively. 'Are you having a party?'

Mrs Chalker snapped her bag shut. 'Never you mind, smarty-pants. What are you doing out so late?'

Mrs Chalker pointed at Alfie with her umbrella. 'You're a funny little fellow. Why is your hat pulled down like that? Why have you got a scarf over your nose? It's hardly freezing, is it? You look like a gangster . . . Or are you feeling guilty about something? Scared to show our face, are we?' She poked Alfie in the stomach with her umbrella. 'Well, speak up! There's something funny about you. I can smell it. Strange things have been happening around here lately. You two wouldn't know anything about it, would you?'

Tim was starting to get fed up with the

old busybody. 'We don't know anything about anything, Mrs Chalker,' he said. 'Alfie's just got a cold, that's all.'

Mrs Chalker kept looking at Alfie as if he was a lost Eskimo, he was wrapped up that well. The lenses of his glasses gleamed in the moonlight.

'Those glasses look familiar,' Mrs Chalker mumbled. Slowly her eyes drifted away from his face, down his coat to his legs, and finally to his . . .

Mrs Chalker screamed.

'Ah, those feet! What kind of feet are they? They're not feet! They're—'

'Slippers,' Tim said quickly. 'Great, aren't they? I've got striped tiger's paws. Alfie got wolf paws. They're lovely and warm, these slippers. Alfie likes them so much he even wears them outside.'

Alfie held his breath while the seconds ticked away. Would Mrs Chalker believe Tim's story? And if she didn't, what then?

'Oh, of course, slippers.' Mrs Chalker gave a very short laugh.

'What did you think they were?' Tim asked.

Mrs Chalker screwed one eye shut. Her other eye had a sly, yellow gleam to it.

'Nothing!' she said. 'I didn't think anything at all.'

In the coop, the chickens started cackling again. Alfie's ears pricked up under his hat. The werewolf hunger started rising up again inside him at the thought of one of those tender, juicy chickens – mmmmmm. But it wasn't allowed. He had to keep himself under control.

'Shut up or I'll wring your necks!' Mrs Chalker yelled at the chicken coop. 'If you ask me, those stupid chickens are all mixed up. What could be causing it?'

She squinted at Alfie.

Tim laid a hand on Alfie's shoulder.

'No idea, Mrs Chalker. We have to go home.'

He pulled Alfie away before she could ask any more strange questions. On the way, he picked up Alfie's boots.

Alfie didn't dare go in through the back door. He was scared that Tim's parents would see him.

'I'll take the drainpipe,' he said.

He clambered up the pipe as quick as anything. Tim watched Alfie disappear over the window ledge and for a moment he felt a pang of jealousy. Being able to climb like that must be amazing – as long as nobody caught you at it, of course.

Fortunately everything had gone well. The three nights of full moon were over and Alfie was safe in his room. Tomorrow he would be an ordinary little boy again and they would have a month to look for that mystery man.

If he exists, that is, Tim thought. Maybe Alfie made him up. Or he'd been sitting there dreaming in the park.

Tim went inside and put Alfie's boots down on the mat in the kitchen. The floor was sopping wet. The pipes under the sink were held together with bandages and plasters.

Tim shook his head and laughed. Dad's swimming trunks hadn't helped, he thought.

Then he heard voices in the living room. Dad's and Mum's and a voice he didn't know.

'So you're absolutely certain,' the voice said. 'You haven't seen a strange kind of wolf anywhere in the neighbourhood?'

24

Mr Collins

Worried, Tim walked into the room.

'Ah, Tim,' Dad said. He was sitting on the sofa next to Mum, wearing a tea cosy on his head. 'Say hello to Mr Collins.'

A man in a raincoat was sitting in one of the armchairs. He had a beard and a black bag. Tim hesitated, then nodded hello.

'Mr Collins is from the RCUPA,' Mum said.

Tim looked at the man suspiciously. 'What's that?' he asked.

'The Reception Centre for Unusual

People and Animals.'

'Oh! And what does a reception centre like that do?'

'We have a splendid collection of Unusual People and Animals,' Mr Collins replied. 'Our latest acquisition was a rare black stork, captured last year at a primary school. We also have a granny who thinks she's a cowboy. She shares her cage with a very large crocodile. It's her best friend. And besides that . . .'

Tim had stopped listening. For a moment he felt dizzy. *Disaster!* flashed through his thoughts. They know. They've come for Alfie.

A werewolf is an unusual person and an unusual animal in one. They're going to lock him up.

What should he do? Warn Alfie so that he could escape? Give Mr Collins a kick? Pretend that he's suddenly come down with a deadly disease so that everyone would panic?

'Mr Collins is here for a neighbourhood survey,' Mum explained. 'Someone from our street rang him up with a strange story.'

'Mrs Chalker,' Dad said, winking at Tim.

'Exactly,' Mr Collins said. 'That lady told me that she saw a white wolf in her garden. A white wolf wearing glasses.'

'Oh,' said Tim.

'We of the RCUPA are extremely interested in wolves with glasses. They're unusual animals. To tell you the truth, I've never even heard of them. But of course we investigate all rumours about unusual animals or people.'

'Oh,' Tim said again. He was so relieved he felt like shouting. The man didn't know anything. He was only doing a survey.

'Mrs Chalker is a nut,' Tim said.

The man from the RCUPA looked shocked.

'Shame on you, Tim,' Dad said with a smile. 'You mustn't say things like that. It's true, but you mustn't say it.'

Mr Collins looked a little confused. He stared at the tea cosy on Dad's head, as if he'd found an unusual person for his reception centre. Then he turned back to Tim.

'You haven't by any chance seen a wolf with glasses, have you?'

Tim nodded.

His parents stared at him in astonishment.

Mr Collins sat up straight. He got a pen and paper out of his bag.

'You're quite sure, son? Where exactly was it?'

Tim smirked and didn't say a word.

'Come on, Tim,' his father said. 'Spit it out. Mr Collins is waiting for an answer and we're very curious as well.'

Tim nodded. A broad smile appeared on his face.

'In a cartoon on TV.'

Mr Collins sighed and put the pen and paper back in his bag. 'Well, if you do happen to see a wolf like that in real life, give us a call. We'll keep a cage free for it, next to our unusual black stork.'

Mum showed Mr Collins out while Dad put the tea cosy back on the teapot.

'There, my head's warm enough now.'

Tim looked at him thoughtfully.

'Dad,' he said at last. 'Why do you always put strange things on your head? And why do you always wear such weird clothes? Normal people don't do stuff like that, do they?'

Dad smiled.

'Normal is so ordinary,' he said. 'I don't want to be the same as everyone else. That's boring.'

Tim hesitated. He was thinking about how strange it was. Alfie didn't want to be different from other people. But that was just what his dad wanted. Then he asked, very carefully, 'Dad?'

'Yes, Tim.'

'If you saw a wolf with glasses, would you call the RCUPA?'

For a long time Dad stared silently at an empty flowerpot on the windowsill. He grabbed the pot, turned it upside down, and put it on his head. Then he looked at Tim and pulled a funny face.

'I think I'd just keep it,' he said. 'Even if it turned out to be a werewolf! That'd be really different!'

25

The Man from the Park

The next morning, Alfie was walking to school with Tim.

'So this Mr Collins really doesn't know that I'm a werewolf?'

'Of course not,' Tim answered. 'He doesn't know anything. He was there because of Mrs Chalker. You really don't need to be scared of Mr Collins.'

'Phew,' Alfie sighed.

He looked around the busy street. Lots of people were on their way to school or work. Suddenly he froze. His heart began to beat faster.

'What is it?' Tim asked.

Alfie pointed across the road.

His voice changed to a whisper. 'That's him, I think.'

'Who?'

'The man from the park.'

Tim stared. Cars and mopeds zoomed past. There were a lot of people on the other side of the road.

'I can't see him,' Tim said. 'I don't even know what he looks like. I've never seen him.'

'There, with the hat and the walking stick. I'm going after him.'

'I'm coming too,' Tim said.

They crossed the road and ran after him, dodging between the people. In the distance Alfie saw the man's hat. He ran even faster. Tim couldn't keep up with him and gave up. Just round the corner, Alfie caught up to the man.

'Excuse me,' he panted.

The man stopped and turned around. He

was wearing dark glasses.

Alfie stared at him for a few seconds. And then at the white stick. He only noticed that now.

'Can I help you?' the man asked in a friendly voice.

'I, I, I . . .' Alfie stammered. 'I thought you were someone else. I made a mistake.' Then he quickly made himself scarce.

'Wow, you can run fast all of a sudden,' Tim said. 'Before, you couldn't even keep up with me. So, was that him?'

Alfie shook his head.

'No, it wasn't the right person, it was a blind man.'

Tim looked at him as they walked into the playground. 'Does this mystery man really exist? You sure he wasn't just a dream?'

'He exists,' Alfie said. 'And I'm going to find him.'

But he didn't sound so sure.

At school things were going well. Nick

Bragman stayed away from Alfie. And he left Tim in peace too. That wasn't all that had changed, as Alfie discovered during P.E.

'On the ropes,' Mr French said.

Alfie had never been good at P.E. And he'd always been especially bad at climbing ropes.

In the gym there were six ropes hanging from a rail on the ceiling. Six children had to take turns climbing while the rest of the class cheered them on.

Alfie was in the last group. He looked at the rope with a sigh. At the bottom there was a big fat knot you could stand on with both feet. Alfie didn't usually get much further than the knot.

'Come on, Alfie,' Mr French said. 'Just try. If you get halfway up, you're a star!'

Alfie nodded. He looked at the rope again. I'm not going to let it beat me, he thought. I climbed up the drainpipe at home, didn't I? I didn't think about it, I just did it.

'Ready?' Mr French called.

He blew hard on a whistle. The kids

grabbed the ropes. They pulled themselves up until they were standing on the knots.

Alfie felt the rope between his hands. And suddenly he knew what to do. He bit into the rope.

His hands grabbed the rope above his head. He pulled himself up.

Bite. Grab. Up.

Bite. Grab. Up.

He went so fast that no one even noticed until Noura, a girl with long black hair, suddenly screamed, 'Hey, Alfie's already at the top!'

All at once everyone in the gym fell silent.

26

Round of Applause

All eyes looked up at the ceiling, where Alfie was holding on to the very top of the rope. Even he was dumbfounded. He saw his classmates' faces with their mouths hanging open in shock.

Mr French was speechless too. His whistle had dropped from between his lips and there was a dazed look in his eyes as if he had just seen a miracle.

The other climbers were only halfway up. They too stared up incredulously and forgot to climb any further.

Alfie clamped the rope between his feet and held on with one hand. He grinned shyly and waved with his free hand. Then he slid down carefully.

All the kids gathered around him when he got to the bottom. Everyone was talking at once.

'How did you do that, Alfie?'

'Have you been taking pep pills?'

'You looked like a rocket, you zoomed up so fast.'

No one paid any attention to the other climbers, who were still up on their ropes. Not even Mr French. He laid a hand on Alfie's shoulder.

'That was extraordinary, Alfie. I didn't know you were so good at climbing. Actually, I didn't think you could climb at all.'

Alfie looked at his teacher shyly.

'I didn't think so either, sir. But all of a sudden I just knew how to do it.'

Mr French thought for a moment.

'When did you get so good at climbing, Alfie?'

Alfie almost said, 'When I turned into a werewolf, sir.' Fortunately, he stopped himself just in time.

'When I turned . . . um, when I turned seven, sir.'

Mr French shook his head. 'I've never known anyone to improve so quickly before. It's extraordinary! Do you think you could do it again, Alfie? You were so fast, I didn't even see it properly. I don't think anyone really saw it.'

'He cheated, of course,' mumbled Vincent. Vincent was the best at sport in the whole class. He was best at long jump, high jump, running and rope climbing. And he was also the worst loser.

Mr French ignored Vincent. 'Try it again, Alfie,' he said calmly.

The other climbers had come back down in the meantime.

'OK,' Alfie said.

He walked over to a rope and grabbed hold of it. Everyone in the gym fell silent again. Alfie looked around. All eyes were on him.

'Here goes,' Alfie said.

He pulled himself up on to the knot.

Bite. Grab. Up.

Bite. Grab. Up.

Mr French and the children blinked. They saw Alfie shoot up the rope like a rocket. In moments he was already back up at the ceiling.

'Incredible,' Mr French whispered with deep awe in his voice. 'That's a star turn, Alfie.'

'See, he's cheating,' Vincent suddenly shouted. 'He bites the rope. I saw it myself.'

Noura gave Vincent a shove. 'So what? It's not against the rules. And anyway that makes it a lot harder than normal climbing.' Her eyes gleamed as she looked at Alfie and she started clapping very loudly.

The other kids followed her example. Everyone started clapping. Even Mr French joined in. Only Vincent sat in the corner scowling.

But no one paid him any attention.

Alfie was the hero of the day.

* * *

After school, Noura came up to Alfie.

'Would you like to come to my birthday party next month?' she asked.

Alfie looked at her, stunned. No one ever asked him to come to their party. Everyone always thought he was a wimp and not worth inviting. That seemed to have changed.

'I'd love to,' he said, and ran off singing.

Maybe the mystery man was right. 'You should be happy with your gift,' he had said.

Today, at least, I am happy, Alfie thought.

'What are you so cheerful about?' Tim asked on the way home.

'I'm glad to be,' sang Alfie, 'I'm glad to be a werewolf like me.'

He climbed – zip-zip – up a tree and dangled from a branch while he sang.

Tim looked at his friend thoughtfully. He's getting a bit too confident, he thought. That could be trouble!

27

Pain

Alfie had never felt so great. Suddenly everything was going well.

Nick Bragman was as meek as a lamb. He didn't dare tell anyone what had happened that night. He was too scared they would all laugh at him. Alfie was suddenly a hero at sport, thanks to the ropes. And soon he'd get to go to Noura's party. Things couldn't have been better.

Weeks went by and Alfie almost forgot about the mystery man.

I don't actually need him, he thought.

Everything is fine the way it is, isn't it? I can stop looking for him.

At last the day of Noura's party had come. Six kids had been invited. They watched *The Lion King* and then they played games.

Alfie was really enjoying himself. Noura smiled at him now and then, and that made him feel even happier.

It was only towards evening that things went wrong. They turned off the lights and lit candles, and then everyone got a piece of cake on a plate with a small silver fork.

'Look how beautiful the moon is.' Noura pointed out through the window. 'It's just like a Chinese lantern.'

Alfie nodded. He brought the silver fork up to his mouth to take a bite of cake and then . . .

Pain! Pain!

A burning pain shot through his body. As if the fork had given him an electric shock.

The fork clattered to the floor and Alfie dropped the plate with the cake on it. Cream splattered all over the rug.

Astonished, Alfie looked at his hands. What had happened? Was it because of the fork?

The pain was already gone.

He looked back at his hands. His nails looked longer. Or was he just seeing things? Suddenly his neck felt itchy. When he scratched it, he felt hair under his collar.

Oh no! thought Alfie as his legs started shaking. It's happening again.

Noura came up to him. 'What's wrong, Alfie? Where's your cake?'

Noura's mother turned on the light and looked at the rug with a frown. 'Do you smear cream over the floor at home too?' she asked as she went to the kitchen to get a cloth.

Alfie turned bright red. He'd ruined the party.

Anxiously, he looked out of the window at the moon. The full moon! He hadn't given it a second thought over the last few days. Oh, how he hated the moon. Now things were going to go wrong again.

'I . . . I've got to go,' Alfie stuttered.

He felt itchy all over his body. What if he turned into a werewolf on the spot? A werewolf that had smeared cream on the carpet. That would be a disaster! Just when Noura was starting to like him.

Nervously, he started to scratch everywhere: his back, his neck, under his arms. He had to twist into all kinds of weird positions.

Noura gave him a worried look. 'Are you all right, Alfie? Aren't you enjoying the party?'

Now the other kids were looking at him too.

Maybe my face is already hairy, thought Alfie. And maybe my ears have already changed.

He covered his face with his hands. He couldn't let them see him like this.

'Yeah, I'm fine, it's great,' he mumbled. He saw white hair emerging from his sleeves. 'But I have to go.'

Like lightning he raced to the coat rack, grabbed his coat and tore out of the door.

On the way home, tears scalded his eyes.

A fool, a fool, he looked a fool! He would always have to hide and run away to avoid getting caught out.

Being a werewolf was horrible.

28

Eyes

Alfie ran all the way home. He went around the back and into the kitchen. Panting, he looked in the mirror. Nothing was happening. His ears were normal. His nose was normal. His face was normal. No hairs in sight.

He had been scared about nothing. He had just imagined it all. That was why he'd felt itchy all over. There wasn't even a white hair poking out of his sleeve. It was just a thread.

He'd run away from the party for no reason. He stamped on the floor angrily.

'Stupid! Stupid! Stupid!'

'What's up with you?' Tim asked.

Alfie jumped. He hadn't heard Tim coming in.

'Nothing,' he said. 'There's nothing wrong with me at all. The only problem is I'm a werewolf.' He sighed deeply.

'Come on,' Tim said. 'Let's spend the whole evening chilling in front of the TV with a bag of crisps.'

Alfie looked at Tim.

'The whole evening? Is that allowed?'

Tim started laughing.

'Sure. Mum and Dad have gone out to see the musical *Peter and the Wolf*. I didn't want to because you couldn't go.'

'So we're home all by ourselves?' Alfie said.

Tim pulled an enormous bag of crisps out from behind his back.

'It's sad, isn't it?' he said grinning.

Tim was stretched out on the sofa watching a horror film on TV. Alfie was sitting on the

armchair with his legs over one of the armrests.

Big letters appeared on the screen. *THE END*.

'Cool film,' Tim said, stretching. 'They should make a book of it. Catch!'

He threw a handful of crisps at Alfie. Alfie didn't catch them. He stared ahead gloomily. The film had hardly got through to him at all.

He was thinking of Noura. He liked her a lot. Running away like that had been really stupid. She was bound to be furious with him and her mother would never forgive him. He had completely wrecked things. Why on earth had he dropped that stupid cake?

Suddenly he sat up straight. He swung his legs over the armrest and put his feet on the floor.

'Silver!' he shouted. 'Now I understand! It was because of the silver fork. The man in the park was right.'

Tim looked at the crisps that had fallen on the carpet. 'A silver fork? You can eat crisps with your fingers, you know. It's not soup or something.'

Alfie shook his head. 'No. I don't mean that.'

He explained what had happened at Noura's party.

'It hurt,' he said. 'Like a burning pain.'

'The fork?' Tim asked.

Alfie nodded. 'Silver is dangerous for werewolves. The mystery man in the park told me that.'

Alfie grabbed the arms of his chair. He looked around the room, his eyes taking in all the silver. In the glass cabinet there were silver pots and jugs. There was a silver tray on the cupboard. They had silver cutlery.

126

There were silver clocks, silver watches, silver rings and silver bracelets.

Tim's mother loved silver. She even collected it.

'I'm surrounded by danger,' Alfie stammered. 'The whole house is full of silver. I only just noticed.'

Tim didn't say a word. He stared at his friend. Alfie's ears had turned pointed and hairy. The hands holding the armrests were covered with white fur, and white hair had started sprouting all over Alfie's face.

'What are you looking at?' asked Alfie.

Tim pointed at Alfie's hands. 'Er...it's that time again, I think, Alfie.'

Alfie held his hands up in front of his face and looked at them. They had turned into paws.

'*Wrow!*' said Alfie.

Tim just nodded. Fascinated, he watched the hair grow out of Alfie's sleeves and the legs of his jeans.

'*Wrow!*' Alfie said again.

Tim still couldn't speak. His eyes widened

as Alfie's socks ripped open and his toes appeared, long and hairy with sharp nails.

High in the sky, from behind a cloud, the full moon watched silently through the window.

There was someone else watching too. A dark figure at the window.

Two gleaming, yellowish eyes peered over the window ledge.

29

Sirens

'I knew it,' Mrs Chalker mumbled while peering in through the window. 'I knew I had to keep my eye on those brats. Especially the one with the glasses. He's a beast. But I'll get him. I've taken measures!'

Silently she slipped out of the garden.

Alfie leapt up. Quickly, he pulled off his socks.

'What are you doing?' Tim asked.

'I'm going away,' Alfie growled.

'Away? Where?'

Tim stared at Alfie as if he had gone mad. Then he saw the tears in Alfie's eyes.

'I dunno. Away. I can't stay here. I'm not normal. I can't even eat cake with a silver fork! I don't want to have to hide for three nights every full moon.'

For a moment Tim was totally astonished. 'But... I don't want you to go away. You're my best friend.'

Suddenly Tim got to his feet. 'I'm coming with you!'

Alfie shook his head. 'I'm going alone, Tim. First to the park. I have to find the mystery man. He's the only one who understands how it all works.'

'But I can help you look, can't I?' Tim asked.

'*Wrow!*' Alfie shook his head. 'You have to stay here with your parents. Maybe I'll find my own mum and dad somewhere. They must love me. Then I won't have to hide all the time.' He scratched his head with a claw. 'I think they must be werewolves too. How else could I be one? But first I have to find that man. He can help me find them.'

Tim felt himself getting desperate. 'But my parents love you too!'

Alfie laughed joylessly. 'They don't know that I'm a werewolf. If they knew . . .' He shook his head. 'No one wants a werewolf around the house.'

He threw his clothes on the chair. 'Bye, Tim,' he growled. 'You'll always stay my best friend.'

Then he turned and ran out of the kitchen.

'Wait, Alfie, wait!' Tim shouted. Tears choked his voice. But the back door slammed shut and Alfie was gone; only his clothes were left behind.

Alfie sucked in the night air. It was as if the moon was smiling at him. High above, the stars were twinkling. Not once did he look back.

He felt a pang of sorrow thinking about Tim. He was his best friend.

Then he shook his head. He really couldn't

stay here. Werewolves weren't welcome anywhere.

A quiet howl rose up out of his throat. His ears drooped sadly. He knew every house on the street. This is the last time I'll see these houses, he thought. I'll never come back here again.

At least I won't miss that creepy old biddy, he thought as he passed Mrs Chalker's house.

Suddenly he froze. There was a racket coming from Mrs Chalker's chicken coop. Cackling and fluttering.

Alfie's ears stood up. What's going on with those chickens? he thought. Every time I go past, they . . . Shall I have a quick look? Just a look. I'm really not going to eat any of them.

He growled softly. The hunger was back, the werewolf hunger.

Just a look, he thought. Or perhaps he'd better not?

But by then he was already in the garden. He couldn't help himself. The chickens cackled louder. Alfie ran his tongue over his teeth.

Mrs Chalker's house was dark. She was probably already asleep, with her feather hat on.

Alfie crept closer on his wolf paws. It's not allowed, he thought. I don't want to bite things. But those thoughts came from Alfie the little boy. And the hunger came from Alfie the werewolf. And the hunger was stronger.

One step closer.

The chickens felt him coming. 'Wolf! Wolf!' they seemed to cackle.

Suddenly Alfie stumbled over a wire.

Then: *CLANG!*

A trap, as hard as steel, slammed shut on his hind leg. Alfie screamed with pain and the next thing he knew a net had landed on top of him. All over the garden, lights started flashing: white, blue, red. ON – OFF – ON – OFF – ON – OFF.

The chicken coop looked like a disco with flickering lights. The chickens cackled like mad things. Sirens blared.

Alfie tried to wrestle free, but just got more and more tangled in the net. His hind leg burnt with pain, searing pain. The trap was made of silver.

Inside Mrs Chalker's house the lights went on.

30

Trapped

The lights kept flashing, but suddenly the blaring sirens fell silent. The door flew open and out stepped Mrs Chalker, wearing her feather hat and holding her umbrella.

'Got ya!' She was mad with delight. 'I've got you, you chicken killer. You fell for my tripwires and my beautiful silver trap,' she screamed.

Alfie lay tangled in the net. He had worked himself into a big knot.

Mrs Chalker approached slowly. The

flashing coloured lights gave her face a ghostly sheen.

'You thought I was crazy, didn't you, sonny? You thought you could hide. But I recognized you from your glasses.' She sneered. 'I wasn't born yesterday. I go to the library. I read books. Don't think I haven't heard of werewolves.'

She came even closer.

Alfie growled with anger and fear. And from the pain in his hind leg.

'Hurts, doesn't it?' Mrs Chalker grinned. 'Silver is the best weapon against werewolves. I know that from TV. In films they shoot werewolves dead with a silver bullet.'

Alfie tried to break free, but each movement hurt even more.

'You're not going anywhere! Just lie there until they come for you. I've called the RCUPA. They're on their way. They're coming to get you. And then they'll lock you up in a silver cage for ever!' Mrs Chalker gave a vicious laugh.

Alfie growled even louder. He tried to

bite a hole in the net.

'Stop that at once!' Mrs Chalker hissed. 'Otherwise I'll jab you.'

She pointed at Alfie with her umbrella. The point gleamed dangerously.

'Guess what that's made of, werewolf cub. Silver. I had it made this afternoon. One false move and I'll run it right through you.'

31

Madder and Madder

Tim stood in the kitchen. He rubbed his face.

What do I do, what do I do? he thought.

There was only one thing he could do. Go after Alfie this minute!

He couldn't possibly let him leave like this. Alfie didn't have anything, he didn't have anyone. He belongs here with us, thought Tim. Werewolf or no werewolf.

Suddenly he remembered what his father had said. That he might just keep a werewolf. Because it would be something really different. Maybe Dad was only joking. But maybe he really meant it. I hope so, thought Tim. Because I'm going to bring Alfie back home.

He ran to the hall and pulled on his shoes. He tied the laces of his right shoe and his left shoe up together, stumbled, unpicked the knots, and pulled his coat on back to front. He opened the door and ran into the broom closet. Wrong door.

He walked backwards into the hall.

Calm down, he thought as he put his coat on the right way round.

This time he used the right door too. He stepped outside and immediately heard a strange wailing, like some kind of alarm. Had there been an accident?

Alfie!

Tim's heart pounded against his ribcage as if it was trying to break free. He ran down the garden path towards the alarm, but it had already stopped.

There were no people out on the street, but strange lights were blinking in the distance. It was at Mrs Chalker's, he saw that straightaway.

Tim walked faster, then even faster, until he was running.

He stopped at Mrs Chalker's garden and saw something horrific. Alfie was wriggling on the ground, caught in a net. Mrs Chalker was bending over him with her umbrella.

Tim stopped thinking. He stormed into the garden.

'Stop that!' he screamed. 'Leave my friend alone.'

Mrs Chalker looked up. She squeezed one eye shut. 'Ah, here's the other one, the accomplice.'

Like lightning she raised her umbrella.

'Stay there, you, you're in it too. One step closer and I'll jab him.'

Tim stood still.

'Don't move,' Mrs Chalker shrieked. 'We'll wait here for the RCUPA together. We don't want any werewolves around here.'

Tim looked at the woman with big, scared eyes. She really is mad! he thought.

Mrs Chalker waved her umbrella menacingly. White froth sprayed from her lips. It was as if she was getting madder and madder.

Under the net, Alfie writhed with pain.

'Lie still, werewolf,' Mrs Chalker commanded.

Alfie growled.

'Want me to teach you a lesson, do you?' Mrs Chalker raised the umbrella up over Alfie with both hands.

'No!' Tim screamed, leaping forward.

But something else beat him to it.

There was a rustling of leaves, the snap of branches. A growling black shape leapt out of the bushes. It shot past Tim in the flickering light and threw itself on Mrs Chalker.

Flaming red eyes glowed, white teeth shone. It was a wolf. A big, black one.

32

Big, Black Wolf

Mrs Chalker screamed when she looked into the eyes of the big, black wolf.

'Wo-wo . . . wa . . .' she said and collapsed silently. She had fainted.

Tim stepped back in fright. With its black coat and gleaming eyes, the big wolf was terrifying. But it didn't even look at Tim. It growled once, then bit through the net that was holding Alfie prisoner.

Snap, snap. A few good bites and Alfie was free.

The wolf sniffed Alfie's rear leg. It flinched

away from the silver trap, then looked at Tim and beckoned with a movement of its head.

Tim understood. The wolf wasn't going to hurt him.

Tim raced over to Alfie. He grabbed the silver trap with both hands. He pulled on its vicious jaws as hard as he could. He strained so hard he felt like his head was going to burst. But the trap wouldn't budge from Alfie's hind leg.

The black wolf watched from a distance unable to do anything to help.

Tim took a deep breath. Open! he thought. Open! Then he pulled again with all his might. The jaws of the trap moved just a little bit away from each other. That was enough. Alfie's hind leg shot out. *Clang!* The trap slammed shut again. But Alfie was free.

Tim wrapped his arms around Alfie's hairy neck.

'*Wrow*,' said Alfie. 'I knew you'd come.'

He closed his eyes and went limp.

The black wolf looked at them and growled softly, 'I told you you were clumsy.'

Just then a car screeched to a halt in front of the house. The doors flew open and Tim's father got out. He was wearing a leather coat, leather trousers, boots and a motorbike helmet. He looked like a pilot from an old-fashioned war film. Mum got out on the other side. They both raced up the garden path.

'Tim,' Dad shouted.

The black wolf disappeared into the darkness before Mum and Dad made it to the chicken coop.

Tim looked up at them. How did they get here all of a sudden? Hadn't they gone to see *Peter and the Wolf*? And now they're going to see Tim and the wolf, he thought.

'We left early,' Mum said, as if she could read his mind. 'It wasn't any fun without you.'

'What happened?' Dad asked in a worried voice.

He squatted next to Tim, who still had his arms wrapped around Alfie.

'It's Alfie . . .' Tim said. 'He's . . . he's a

werewolf. I mean, he's dressed up as a werewolf. He's . . .' His voice broke. He looked at his parents with tear-filled eyes. 'They're coming to get him, the RCUPA. They're going to take him away and lock him up. Mrs Chalker called them.'

In the distance they heard the sound of another car.

33

The RCUPA

Tim's father and mother looked at each other. They didn't hesitate for a moment.

'Quick, get that poor boy in the car,' Mum said.

Dad picked up Alfie and carried him to the car. He laid him on the back seat and slammed the door.

The car from the RCUPA pulled up right behind theirs. Four men jumped out, with Mr Collins leading the way. They were weighed down with ropes, chains, a straitjacket and a cage.

'Where is it, where is it?' Mr Collins shouted sounding very excited.

Tim's father took off his helmet. Under it he was wearing a cap.

'What are you talking about?' he asked.

'The werewolf. Mrs Chalker called us. She said she'd caught it next to her chicken coop.'

'Exactly,' Tim's father said. 'Follow me.'

Quickly he gave the car keys to Mum. 'Do you think you can drive that little bit home, honey?' he whispered.

'I'm sure I'll manage,' Mum said. 'There's always a first time for everything . . .'

Dad led the men into the garden.

In the meantime Mum hurried Tim over to the car. 'We'll be off home,' she called out.

'OK, I'll walk home when I'm done,' Dad said, shepherding the men further into Mrs Chalker's garden.

Mum and Tim got into the car. She stuck the key into the ignition and tried to start the engine. On her third attempt it started

and jolted off down the road.

'Look,' Dad said to the RCUPA men. 'That's the chicken coop. And this is Mrs Chalker.'

The men stared disbelievingly at the blinking lights decorating the chicken coop. And at the woman, who was stretched out on the ground as if she was blind drunk, with her feather hat still stuck firmly on her head.

'And the werewolf?' Mr Collins asked very quietly.

Tim's father shook his head.

'Mrs Chalker is an unusually strange person.' He winked at Mr Collins. 'Unusually strange, if you get my meaning.' He dropped his voice to a whisper. 'I'm sure she'd be a beautiful acquisition for the Reception Centre for Unusual People and Animals.'

'Ooh,' said Mr Collins. His face lit up. He suddenly gazed with great interest at the unconscious Mrs Chalker.

'She's one of a kind,' Dad whispered secretively. 'A rare opportunity. I mean, that woman sees werewolves all over the place. Unusual, don't you think?' He nudged Mr Collins with his elbow. 'And something else: that feather hat. We suspect that it has merged to her head. More than that, we suspect that those feathers actually grow out of her head, maybe even directly out of her brain. Now tell me, is that unusual or isn't it?'

Mr Collins's face glowed with excitement. 'Don't say another word,' he shouted. 'OK, guys, wrap the package. Slip her into the straitjacket and throw her in the car. We'll put her in the cage next to the black stork.'

The men were very keen workers. When Mrs Chalker opened her eyes, with difficulty, she was already in the straitjacket in the back of the car. Her head wobbled back and forth.

'Another werewolf,' she said. 'A black one, enormous, a whopper.'

The men from the RCUPA nodded and smiled.

'Never you mind, Mrs Chalker, never you mind now.'

Watching the car drive off, Tim's father smiled too. Then he walked home.

Turning into a werewolf! he thought, feeling a little jealous. That's something that really is cool. Wow, what a rush! It beats just dressing up. It's a *real* transformation. If I could just learn how to do that . . .

34

Different

Alfie opened his eyes. He was lying on the sofa.

For a few seconds the living room was a big blur. Then he saw Tim and his parents. All three of them were looking at him with worried faces.

Alfie still felt a little weak but he was getting over it. The pain in his leg was fading.

He raised his arm. He could move it all right. Then he saw his hand: a white, hairy paw. Suddenly he realized that he was still a werewolf.

And everyone was sitting there looking at him! Tim's father and mother . . .

Alfie shot up.

Immediately they pushed him back down.

'Take it easy, Alfie,' Dad said. 'Relax. We know all about it. Tim has already told us everything.'

Tim? Had Tim betrayed him?

Alfie's eyes flashed back and forth between Tim and his parents.

'It's OK, Alfie,' Dad said.

'But . . . but I'm a werewolf,' Alfie growled. 'I'm not normal, I'm different from—'

'It's fantastic,' Dad said. 'I love things that are different, don't you know that yet? I wish I could do what you can do.'

Tim burst out laughing. 'Look what Dad's wearing now, Alfie. A wrinkly bathing cap.'

His father raised an eyebrow. 'That's not a bathing cap, son. That's my head. I shaved my head.'

'Oh, sorry,' Tim said.

Mum laid a hand on Alfie's paw. 'See, Alfie, you're actually fairly normal. You're only different at full moon. My dear husband is different all the time. I love things that are different. That's why I love him. And I love you too.'

Alfie swallowed.

'What I was wondering . . .' Tim said. 'Who was that black—'

Just then the doorbell rang.

Tim opened the door and jumped back immediately.

A hat, a long coat, a walking stick. Standing there in the darkness was the mystery man. All Tim could make out was his gleaming eyes.

The man touched the brim of his hat. He was wearing black gloves.

'May I come in for a moment?'

His voice was scary, but Tim nodded.

They went through to the living room. Tim's parents looked at the strange man with surprise.

'Don't be frightened,' he said.

35

Wrow!

The man took off his hat. A black wolf's head appeared, with flashing teeth.

'You?' Alfie said.

Tim took a quick step backwards.

Mum and Dad looked at their guest a little anxiously. Two werewolves in one house was a bit too much.

The black werewolf pulled off his gloves. Tim swallowed when he saw the big black paws. Now he knew what was hidden under that long black coat.

'Who . . . who are you?' Dad asked.

The wolf grinned, displaying a mouth full of sharp teeth. Pitch-black eyes stared at Alfie.

'I'm your grandpa!'

Alfie shot up, ignoring the pain in his leg.

'My grandpa? I knew it must be in the family. My parents must be werewolves too then!'

Grandpa Werewolf shook his head. Groaning, he sat down on a chair. His coat gaped open, revealing hairy legs.

'No, Alfie, your parents aren't werewolves. But I knew you would become one. That's how it's passed on in our family. Not from father to son, but from grandfather to grandson.'

Alfie didn't understand. 'What happened to my parents then?'

Grandpa Werewolf growled. 'When you were three, I told them. I thought it was better for them to find out in time, so they could get used to it. I explained very carefully that you would become a werewolf on your seventh birthday. Just like I did.'

Alfie got a strange premonition.

'What happened then?' he asked, with a strange trembling in his growly little voice.

Grandpa Werewolf gave an angry snort. 'They weren't happy. They thought it was horrible. They packed their bags and ran away that very night.'

The old werewolf stared hard at Alfie.

'They were weaklings, Alfie. Not worthy of being your parents.'

Tim's mother wrapped an arm around Alfie. 'Oh, you poor boy, dumped, just like that.'

'Exactly,' Grandpa Werewolf growled. 'Disgraceful. That's why I went looking for new parents for you. Better parents.' He pointed at Tim's father and mother. 'And that's where this family came into it. I went looking for parents who were special. Parents who loved things that were different and who would love you too. Fortunately, I found them. By the looks of things, it was the right choice.'

A big smile appeared on Dad's face. His bald head gleamed with pride.

'I laid you here on the doorstep at night,' Grandpa said. 'Then I rang the bell and ran away.'

'Oh, was that you?' Tim's mother said. She was still holding Alfie and now she ran her fingers through the fur on his head. 'Why did you run away?'

Grandpa Werewolf scratched himself behind the ear with his claws.

'I didn't want to scare you straightaway. It was full moon and I looked just like I do now.'

It turned into a very enjoyable evening despite Alfie's sore leg.

Tim's mother threw all her silver straight into the rubbish bin. 'There, that won't bother you any more, Alfie,' she said. 'We won't let another sliver of silver into the house.'

Alfie had lots of questions to ask his grandfather. Especially about the werewolf hunger, because he didn't want to bite anyone. Not even chickens.

'But sometimes the hunger gets so strong,' he said.

'No problem,' Grandpa Werewolf growled. 'Just make sure you've got some raw steaks in the fridge come full moon. Then the hunger will be over before you know it. Now that you mention it, I'm feeling peckish myself.'

Mum ran straight to the fridge and grabbed a steak. Grandpa and Alfie gobbled it up.

'And that card of the Big Bad Wolf, Grandpa? Did you send that too?' Alfie asked with his mouth full.

Grandpa sniggered and burped loudly. 'Lovely steak, thank you. Nice and bloody.'

Dad just looked on silently, loving every minute of it.

'That card?' Grandpa said. 'It was a joke. I wanted to prepare you. And in the meantime I kept my eye on you. That's why I was there in time this evening.' Grandpa wiped his jaws and stood up.

'Oh, do you have to go already?' Alfie looked at Grandpa imploringly. 'There's so much I want to know. Can't you stay here?'

Dad rested one hand on Alfie's shoulder. 'Yes, can't you stay here? You're very welcome.' Dad looked almost as imploring as Alfie. 'You see, I'd like to know more. Much more. About that changing and how exactly it works. With the moon and all that.'

Grandpa Werewolf shook his head. 'I don't fit into a normal household. I don't feel at home with people any more.'

'Where do you live then, Grandpa?' Alfie asked.

The old werewolf had already opened the door. He pointed off into the distance with his stick. 'Faraway, in the woods, under the moon.' He looked at Alfie and winked. 'You see, I always look like this.'

'Always?' Alfie growled.

Dad's mouth dropped.

'You mean you never become human any more?'

Grandpa Werewolf nodded. 'That was my choice. You can do that if you're very old and have already changed form many, many times. The forest is better than an old people's home. I love living a wild life. I only need these clothes when I come into town to avoid attracting too much attention.'

'Cool!' Dad said, sighing deeply.

'I'll take you with me sometime, Alfie,' Grandpa promised. 'On a night with a beautiful full moon. The two of us can run through the woods together.'

Dad sighed even more deeply.

Then they all waved goodbye to Grandpa Werewolf. But only after he had promised to come often to visit.

Inside, the phone was ringing. Tim answered.

'Alfie, it's for you. Noura.'

Alfie limped over to the phone as fast as

he possibly could.

'Hi, Alfie, this is Noura. Would you like to come over to play tomorrow?'

Alfie pressed the receiver against his mouth. *'Wrow!'*

**Read on for a sneak peek at
FULL MOON,
the next Alfie the Werewolf
adventure...**

'You, stop!'

Alfie Span didn't stop and he didn't look back at the man who was chasing him in the dark on a motorbike. He kept running as fast as he could. The man had a big head of bushy hair and a big moustache and he was wearing a big leather coat. He roared over the pavements and swerved between the parked cars, the beam of his headlight zigzagging across the street.

Alfie shot from left to right, but the light kept following him. His heart was pounding in his chest. His tongue was hanging out of his mouth.

'Tired, eh?' the man yelled. 'I'll get you!'

But Alfie ducked out of the way and hid in

the shadows. Panting, he looked from left to right. Where could he go? He was worn out and his stomach was full because he'd just stuffed himself. That was why he couldn't run fast enough. He looked up at the full moon in desperation. And immediately stepped in a puddle, splashing water up into his eyes.

'I'll get you, eh, you horrible hen hunter,' the man shouted behind him.

The moon disappeared behind a black cloud. Rain pattered down on the roofs of the cars and the street turned gleaming black. The next thing Alfie knew, a bright light was glaring in his eyes. He flinched and covered his face.

'I've got you now!' he heard.

Alfie saw a black silhouette on a motorbike.

The man jerked the handlebars, making the motorbike rear up like a horse. Then he pulled a club out from under his coat. Alfie looked around and shrank. There was nowhere to run. The motorbike towered over him as the man swung the club over his head. Things were looking bad for Alfie, but that was just for a second.

The rain had made the road so slippery that the back wheel slipped. The motorbike skidded and fell, sending the man rolling over the road and the club bouncing on to the pavement. The back wheel screeched as it spun around in the air.

For a moment Alfie stood there gaping. He could hardly believe he'd escaped.

'Run, you idiot!' he growled to himself.

He glanced back one last time at the furious man, who was picking himself up, then ran off on all fours, as fast as he could.

'Eh, stop, you nasty little wolf.'

The roar of the motorbike started up again as Alfie ran around a corner. Someone grabbed him. Two hands pushed him to the ground. Something came down on top of him.

'Quick, get up and put this coat on fast,' a voice hissed. Alfie's heart leapt.

'Tim! What are you doing here? I—'

'No time.' Tim sounded hurried. 'Stand on your hind legs. Stick your forepaws in the sleeves, quick.'

He helped Alfie into the long raincoat as the roar of the motorbike came closer. Tim pulled a baseball cap down over Alfie's head and wrapped a scarf around his neck and chin, so that only his glasses were visible. The rain was still beating down. Water was dripping out of Alfie's tail, which was sticking out slightly under the coat. Tim's hair was sopping wet too.

'Come on, let's get home,' he said.

A beam of white light swept over them and the throbbing motorbike stopped just in front of them.

'Eh, boys, wait a sec, eh?'

Tim held up one hand to keep the bright light out of his eyes. Alfie stayed as quiet as a mouse and looked the other way. The man on the motorbike wiped his nose with his arm and sniffed loudly.

'Did you see a wolf run past here? A little white one, eh? With glasses.'

Tim cocked an eyebrow and twisted his face into a crooked grin. 'A wolf with glasses, you say?' He snorted with exaggerated laughter.

'There's no need to laugh at me, eh?' the man growled. 'There was a white wolf in my henhouse. It was wearing glasses! And it ate one of my hens. A nice fat one, eh?'

'A fat white wolf with glasses?' Tim asked.

'No, a fat hen. I was going to eat it myself for Christmas, eh?'

The headlight was still shining on Tim and Alfie. The man studied them and sniffed again. Rainwater dripped from his moustache.

'Maybe your friend saw something, eh?' he asked.

Alfie didn't say a word. His glasses were covered with raindrops but he was too scared to wipe the lenses. He hoped the man wouldn't look down at his feet.

The man peered at him. 'What are you being so quiet about, eh?'

He got off his motorbike. 'I asked you something, pea-brain. You deaf or what? Show your face, eh?' He lunged at the scarf. Alfie shrank back.

'No...'